Gone

The Missing Years of Bjorn Esterday

Book 04

Courtroom

2031

Wynter Sommers

Wynter Sommers

This work is registered with the UK Copyright Service, in accordance with the Copyright, Designs and Patents Act 1988
All rights reserved 284718038 for

GONE: The Missing Years of Bjorn Esterday

USA Copyright © 2015 GJ dePillis
© TXu002023789 and TXu002010532 / 2016

Library of Congress Control Number: 2021936597

Published by Pure Force Enterprises, Inc.
California, USA
Since 2002

INGRAM

INGRAM® Distribution

ISBN 13: 978-1-7184-0033-7
ISBN 10: 1-7184-0033-0

DEDICATION

To those who feel strongly about truth, justice, and the integrity of America; your honorable actions make us proud.

To those who wonder if their daily choices matter; your small decisions impact generations to come.

To those everyday people who don't think they have what it takes; your perseverance and strive for the extraordinary, makes the impossible a reality.

To those who have failed; know you will make it and tomorrow will be better.

Your dreams today become our future tomorrow.
Thank you for everything you do.

Bjorn Esterday
Was Not Born Yesterday
Series

Firebrand (15 Volumes+Conversation Station Book)
Edges (9 Stories +Conversation Station Book)
Gone (24 Stories + Conversation Station Book +
Longfellow Journal for 26 books in Gone set)

Bjorn EDGES Series
EDGES Book 1-Swift Encounter
EDGES Book 2-Rousing Attack
EDGES Book 3-One Foot Under
EDGES Book 4-Earthshake
EDGES Book 5-Broken String
EDGES Book 6-Key Witness
EDGES Book 7-Who is She?
EDGES Book 8-Vanish
EDGES Book 9-Chase or Die

Bjorn Series Alternate Reading Plan

1st	Edges Book 1		25th	Gone Book 11
2nd	Edges Book 2		26th	Firebrand Vol 10
3rd	Gone Book 1		27th	Gone Book 12
4th	Firebrand Vol 1		28th	Gone Book 13
5th	Edges Book 3		29th	Firebrand Vol 11
6th	Firebrand Vol 2		30th	Gone Book 14
7th	Gone Book 2		31st	Gone Book 15
8th	Gone Book 3		32nd	Firebrand Vol 12
9th	Firebrand Vol 3		33rd	Gone Book 16
10th	Gone Book 4		34th	Gone Book 17
11th	Firebrand Vol 4		35th	Firebrand Vol 13
12th	Gone Book 5		36th	Gone Book 18
13th	Gone Book 6		37th	Gone Book 19
14th	Gone Book 25-		38th	Edges Book 5
	Longfellow's Journal		39th	Edges Book 6
15th	Edges Book 4		40th	Gone Book 20
16th	Firebrand Vol 5		41st	Gone Book 21
17th	Gone Book 7		42nd	Edges Book 7
18th	Firebrand Vol 6		43rd	Gone Book 22
19th	Gone Book 8		44th	Firebrand Vol 14
20th	Firebrand Vol 7		45th	Firebrand Vol15 (End)
21st	Gone Book 9		46th	Edges Book 8
22nd	Firebrand Vol 8		47th	Edges Book 9(End)
23rd	Gone Book 10		48th	Gone Book 23
24th	Firebrand Vol 9		49th	Gone Book 24(End)

ACKNOWLEDGMENTS

We acknowledge those who actively build peace. We acknowledge all the selfless talent which contributed to creating meaningful tokens of consideration and sharing. We acknowledge that every person has a daily choice of right or wrong... and we thank you for choosing the right, good, honorable path filled with integrity because that is the difficult and brave path. Small choices today become lasting monuments of loving hope tomorrow.

HOW TO INTERPRET THE CHAPTER TITLES

How to read this book: The title has two numbers. The number on the left is the chapter order in this book. The number on the right of "chapter" is the consecutive continuous chapter in the entire series. The number in parentheses is the year and the rest is a chapter title, sometimes sharing which location the chapter takes place.

For example, below is a chapter which appears in GONE Book #03. It is chapter 6, but GONE continuous saga chapter 13. The action takes place in the year 2030 in the location of Brio in the Gardens. The year is in parenthesis.

6 CHAPTER 13: (2030) BRIO: GARDENS

CONTENTS

0 Settings 0

  Locations 0

  Characters 0

0 PREFACE 1

1 CHAPTER 14: (2031) BRIO: COURTROOM: JURY & ZOR HEAR BJORN'S TESTIMONY 3

2 CHAPTER 15: (2031) BRIO: COURTROOM - ZOR EXPLAINS THE GAMES OF BRIO TO BJORN 13

3 CHAPTER 16: (2031) BRIO: COURTROOM: RECESS ENDS- TRIAL RESUMES 17

4 CHAPTER 17: (2031) BRIO: COURT: RESUMES 24

5 CHAPTER 18: (2030) BRIO: ESCAPE POD:PAT AND BJORN TRY TO ESCAPE FROM BRIO   43

8 What Just Happened? 62

9 Did You Know... 63

10 Vocabulary 68

Settings

Locations

- **AromaX**: City of fragrance & fashion
- **Courtly City**: City of solar & other technical products. Bjorn Esterday and Sarah Paradise live here.
- **Brio**: Underwater village

Characters

- **Dr. Lou Pole Linden**: Research assistant to Otto Mattick in the AromaX labs
- **Otto Mattick**: The Mattick family is an elite class in the city of AromaX
- **Topliner**: The relative of Otto
- **Georgia Peach**: Fellow teacher at Sarah Paradise's school.
- **Sarah Paradise**: Teacher and met Bjorn Esterday in EDGES series
- **Bjorn Esterday**: Reporter at the Daily Memo in Courtly City and with a mistaken identity now a resident at Brio.
- **Pat Seeds**: Garden-keeper in Brio
- **Zor**: Manager of Brio
- **Watson**: Charismatic motivational speaker
- **Lou Pole Linden**: Works in the AromaX labs
- **Tres**: Works with Watson
- **Charlie Horse:** The victim. Otto Mattick is accused of killing Mr. Horse

0 PREFACE

Opportunity. Determination. Curiosity. How will that help Bjorn in a courtroom?

Opportunity. Topliner and Otto made their intentions known. They found an opportunity to escape and they take it. Lou Pole Linden revealed his true character.

Determination. Meanwhile, in a distant land, we see Longfellow and his growing team.

Curiosity. Back in Courtly City, Sarah Paradise and Georgia Peach go out, but something happens at the Courtly Train Station where paths cross with Topliner and Otto. Is this chance happening innocuous or will it impact Sarah's future?

At the same time, we see that the clever Watson team is heading out of Courtly City and on their way to sell new products to a fresh audience.

Meanwhile, Lou Pole Linden contacts Watson about the Otto Mattick courtroom trial. Will Bjorn Esterday finally convince those in Brio that he is not Otto Mattick?

How will the actions of others converge to impact Bjorn? How do the situations in your life which are outside of your control work together to impact you?

1 CHAPTER 14: (2031) BRIO: COURTROOM: JURY & ZOR HEAR BJORN'S TESTIMONY

"The gaps between Zor's visits meant that the courtroom trial had dragged on for some time. Bjorn wondered if this court was really interested in justice. He wondered how much time had really passed. He wondered what his friends and coworkers at the Daily Memo newspaper of Courtly City were doing at this very moment. He wondered if any of them missed him.

Here, he had a possible friend in Pat Seeds. Bjorn didn't know if Pat was male or female or perhaps living underwater made one gender neutral.

When it was announced that Zor would return and court would resume, Bjorn felt confident he could prove his innocence and...

...somehow get out of this place and get home.

Bjorn's first day, actually taking an active part in the underwater Brio court, finally arrived. Today was the day, Bjorn had been told, when he could defend himself against the murder charge, the murder of Charlie Horse.

The flowing golden robes of Zor had swished, indicating that every individual should take a seat. This was Bjorn's second time in the glass underwater courtroom of Brio. Now, Bjorn noticed other residents were walking around outside as if eager to view the show.

Zor notified the jury to come to obedient attention.

Bjorn also sat. Zor pressed the pedal near the defendant's chair. Automatically, iron restraints clamped into place to bind Bjorn.

"Is this really necessary?" Bjorn asked Zor, cutting him off mid breath before Zor could address the jury.

Bjorn continued, "I have not run. I've willingly helped Pat Seeds in the garden. Why would I run, now? Where would I go? I am here to prove the innocence of Otto Mattick...and of Bjorn Esterday."

Zor, ignoring Bjorn, turned away and addressed the jury.

"You have all seen the disturbing images where Charlie Horse became insane before dying. We believe the arrival of this stranger induced that insanity and that this man, Otto Mattick, killed Charlie Horse."

Bjorn Esterday firmly said, "Sir, my

name is Bjorn Esterday. I am not Otto Mattick."

"Silence, Prisoner!" Zor barked. The courtroom buzzed with excitement. Pat Seeds quietly slipped out of the court room. Bjorn could see Pat through the transparent walls, waiting outside.

Zor addressed the jury to remind them of the rules, and then turned to Bjorn saying, "Mr. Mattick. We have permitted you to investigate your own case. You may rise to present your findings."

Zor pressed the pedal which released the defendant's restraints. Bjorn got up from his chair and now turned toward the large structure behind him.

He saw that the image of a face was beginning to protrude out of the tiny cube. After a moment he realized the projected face was on an inflated balloon, which served as structure to give it a three dimensional look. The face was that of Watson.

Bjorn pondered about the purpose of this display. Watson was the landlord of this underwater retreat which accuses its residents of murder.

The projected image began to speak, and addressed Bjorn with, "Proceed, Mr. Mattick, with your defense."

Bjorn realized that if this was only Watson's image, then Watson himself must still be on the surface.

Bjorn looked back at Zor.

Zor seemed to be nervous. Bjorn then glanced through the transparent wall and saw Pat Seeds still waiting. The jury was growing restless. Bjorn realized trying to argue who he really was would be pointless. Even the projected balloon face leader thought he was this Otto Mattick and deserving of some awful fate.

Bjorn inhaled and then said, "I have had the opportunity to observe my quarters as well as those of Charlie Horse. I have done my research, as Zor permitted me. The illustrious Zor told me from the first day of my incarceration that everything is recorded. So, I assumed that the actual death of Charlie Horse was also recorded."

The projected image of Watson snapped, "We have already reviewed this image from the visual recall devices."

Zor interrupted Bjorn, "When I arrived in the portal chute, I was not informed that you had seen the visual recall. Who permitted this?"

In response to Zor's question, Bjorn's guard stood up.

The Brio guard said, "Zor, as I prepared your portal chute for your arrival from the surface, I believe Otto Mattick was being given access to the visual recall room. I believe Pat Seeds aided Otto Mattick in finding the footage associated with the night of Charlie Horses' death," the guard quickly added. Then, in a lighter tone he said, "Oh, and it seems that the portal chute seals might be due for some preventative maintenance repairs."

Bjorn took a step forward. "I was told never to touch any individual here, and I have abided by that rule. I do feel I am entitled to touch the evidence of the night in question. Especially the VR images from the Visual Recall room. Any objections from the Jury?"

The jury shook their heads.

The projected image of Watson rolled its eyes as he said to Zor, "It won't change anything. Let him proceed." The projected image actually yawned.

Zor addressed the guard with a bored wave of flowing robes, dismissing him with, "Go tend to your duties or maintenance or repairs of whatever you said."

The guard marched from the Brio courtroom to resume his post.

Bjorn turned away from the floating

balloon, which acted as the canvas for Watson's projected image, and faced the glass courtroom jury, instead.

Bjorn continued, "Upon reviewing the VR images, I noticed that Charlie Horse was sleeping in his cot, in his confined locked room, as Zor had ordered earlier. Then, Mr. Horse got up as if to confront an intruder. Then he is seen clutching his throat. In one frame, just one, I could see the outline of a knife. This knife was only visible because of the blood from Mr. Horse's neck, which temporarily coated the weapon."

Zor took a sudden step forward, "You saw a knife?"

"No," Bjorn corrected, "I saw the outline of a knife. Briefly. because of the blood, I was able to see the outline of the weapon. Charlie Horse didn't go insane that night. Something frightened him."

One of the jury stood up, "Who or what held the knife?"

Zor informed Bjorn, "You may respond. The Jury can ask you questions at any time, Mr. Mattick."

Bjorn replied to the juror, "It did not appear as if the knife was held by anybody."

The juror replied, "Then you must have caused the insanity and killed Charlie Horse."

"Please," Bjorn calmly stated, "Let me finish."

Zor's flowing robes signaled the Juror to resume the seated position.

Bjorn continued, "There was an intruder, but your cameras did not fully record his or her image."

Zor furrowed his brow. "We don't use magic as a defense, Mr. Mattick. If you maintain there was a physical entity, that entity's image would have been captured on the VR."

"I maintain," Bjorn stated with irrefutable logic, "that the image was somehow altered, thereby removing the identity of the real perpetrator from the Visual Recall recording."

Zor whooshed over to Bjorn so quickly that it seemed as if he had levitated as his robes rolled against the air currents.

Zor whispered to Bjorn, "If you prove your innocence too soon, this game will be dull. You recall the agreement you signed."

Bjorn Esterday tried to figure out what document Zor was referring to. Bjorn struggled to make sense of this underwater world.

2 CHAPTER 15: (2031) BRIO: COURTROOM - ZOR EXPLAINS THE GAMES OF BRIO TO BJORN

Bjorn had to focus on this trial....if it was a trial... What document had he supposedly signed? After some time of evident confusion, the Watson balloon instructed those in the Glass Courtroom of Brio to take a recess.

The cube, which had been projecting the image of Watson onto a floating balloon, now seemed to control the process of deflating. Bjorn, not completely sure who was in charge, figured this must be a break in the proceedings.

Bjorn motioned to Zor and asked, "I don't understand. What document did Otto Mattick sign?"

Zor swooshed around with a dramatic flair.

"Watson is still promoting our paradise, and part of the biggest attraction is entertainment. Right now, you and this trial, are the entertainment, Mr. Mattick. Your squirming reactions during this trial for murder are hugely entertaining, Mr. Mattick. Your contract stipulates that in exchange for us keeping you alive, you promise to keep all of Brio entertained. You are doing a fine job, so don't conclude too quickly."

"Otto Mattick signed or ...I mean, he agreed to that?" Bjorn Esterday asked, still refusing to succumb to the pressure that everybody in Brio thought Bjorn Esterday was this Otto Mattick.

Zor swished as he stated, "You would

prefer to be a live resident under water instead of a corpse underground, would you not, Mr. Mattick?"

"You mean," Bjorn asked, "even if I am proven innocent in this trial, it doesn't matter?"

Bjorn thought to himself that this had never been about justice... Finding the truth. If they are willing to take some talking balloon seriously, he could be sure that Brio residents had no idea what justice was really about. They were actually peddling a trial as a form of entertainment to sell this underwater timeshare.

"As long as Watson can sell beds in this biosphere, you make us more money alive than dead," Zor shrugged, smiling. "If you finish this trial too quickly, then we will have to simply accuse you of something else. For example, as another form of entertainment, you may have witnessed a breakdown of the pumps. We deliberately do not maintain the infrastructure so that continual breakdowns provide a diversion for the residents of Brio. Another form of entertainment, Mr. Mattick."

Zor suddenly spun in an elaborate circle, causing his robes to flare as light, streaming through the surrounding waters, reflected off the golden fabric, casting splashes of rainbow flecks around the courtroom. Abruptly, he struck a dramatic pose as a grand finale to his little dance performance and smiled saying, "See? Entertainment."

Bjorn said to himself with startling realization, "this is insane. I've got to get out."

3 CHAPTER 16: (2031) BRIO: COURTROOM: RECESS ENDS- TRIAL RESUMES

Bjorn noticed the balloon was starting to inflate again, which, Bjorn reasoned, probably meant the trial was about to resume.

Pat Seeds slipped inside the courtroom and approached Bjorn Esterday, who was still un-restrained, but was instructed to remain standing at the defendant's chair.

Pat smiled.

"Pat," Bjorn Esterday started, "I don't see my room guard. Is he coming back?"

"I'm not sure, Bjorn," Pat whispered, then quickly added, "Mr. Otto Mattick, isn't this fun? You are doing a very good job."

Bjorn huskily whispered, "Pat Seeds. I need you to get me out of here."

Pat smiled patiently. "Zor said you are not to go to the surface. Oh! I just remembered I had an apricot teacup poodle named Butch."

Bjorn, desperate, replied, "Pat, I need you to focus. I need you to get me…"

Pat day-dreamily stepped over Bjorn's words, "Butch was eight inches tall like the birthday cake with the chocolate paw prints they gave me when I turned twelve in the unmonitored district of Rough-N-Ready..."

Bjorn took a deep breath and whispered, "Pat Seeds! Please! Zor just told me it doesn't matter if I am innocent or not. If this trial isn't about justice that means they will execute me for entertainment."

Pat, now listening, looked down, "Oh, that is not right. Trials are always about finding out the truth."

"Not for Zor and Watson," Bjorn insisted. "I was born on the surface and I plan to die up there on the surface, not down here."

Pat slowly spun around, but with far less flair than Zor had just done earlier. Bjorn was perplexed.

Pat sang softly while gesturing like a conductor to an imaginary chorus, "This day of your birth, brings great mirth, 'cuz you're on earth, Otto Otto Otto. Past, present, then go forth. We honor your birth."

Bjorn snapped at Pat, "It's not my birthday! Focus, Pat! I need you to take this seriously."

Others in the courtroom started to look at Bjorn as Pat seemed to suddenly wake up. Pat, frowning, looked directly at Bjorn as if he had been rudely inattentive.

Pat said, "You sing your name three times to represent the past, then present, then future... but forth is the closest thing that rhymes with birth...so...Sing with me..."

Bjorn lowered his voice, "Get me to the portal chute that Zor arrived in....the one the guard mentioned earlier."

Pat replied softly, "But, Otto Mattick,

you are guilty. It would not be right to interfere with an execution if you are guilty. The way this trial is going, you are guilty."

Bjorn glanced at the balloon judge, now nearly inflated and almost plump enough to have the image of Watson's face projected onto it.

Bjorn snapped, "Pat, you helped me investigate…gather the evidence to prove my innocence…"

Pat nodded with a smile. "That was fun. I've never done that before."

Bjorn shook his head. Then, leaning forward to Pat Seeds whispered, "Recall whatever morals you had on the surface. Is it right to send an innocent man to his death just for fun?"

Pat now adopted a somber expression and looked down.

Bjorn urgently persisted in a whisper, "If you are satisfied that I'm innocent, will you help me?”

“Help you?” Pat mused softly.

“No day dreaming,” Bjorn snapped his fingers to get Pat Seed’s attention, “I need you to pay attention ...You are not a robot which must swallow the garbage Zor spits out. ...think, listen, and you decide what is true and objectively just....OK?”

Bjorn was feeling uneasy that Pat Seeds, an unbalanced wretchedly sad personality, was his only hope.

Would Pat help him or was Pat Seeds too brainwashed to disobey the capricious rules of Brio?

Zor glided back into the courtroom. Bjorn looked down, thinking hard.

The balloon, which emanated from the cube-base, was now fully inflated. What had Zor called it? A Bonitor?

“Bonitor.” Bjorn breathed to himself.

The Bonitor's projected image finally blinked onto the surface of the smooth inflated floating pillow.

Watson's two-dimensional face projected onto the floating balloon monitor appeared bored. Outside the transparent walls of this courtroom, even more residents were gathering. This was their entertainment. The curious residents were oblivious and uncaring if Bjorn was a willing or unwilling participant. Choice was not an option in Brio. Their entertainment was the top priority.

This trial was indeed entertaining

4 CHAPTER 17: (2031) BRIO: COURT: RESUMES

From up above, sun shafts beamed down through the waters surrounding the transparent dome of Brio's courtroom. Sea creatures of all sizes darted about.

Zor appeared to map out where the brightest beam of light would hit the floor, so he made sure to step into nature's spotlight, gazing at his golden fabrics with a smile.

Bjorn looked around.

Objectively, this place was beautiful, however, any place where you are held against your will, becomes a repugnant dungeon no matter how hypnotically ethereal the environment. Bjorn would never see water the same way after this. He was disgusted by how much power that floating head balloon, he now knew as Judge Watson the Bonitor, held over these residents.

Zor swished dramatically at Bjorn and cautioned, "You may proceed with your self-defense story." Then Zor leaned toward him and winked at Bjorn, adding, "Slowly, now."

"Of course your enormous, Zor," Bjorn returned.

Bjorn bowed respectfully, first to Zor, next to the balloon face of Watson, and finally to the jury. He noted the growing crowds gathering outside the transparent walls and gave them a little wave. The audience, surprised at being able to interact with a prisoner directly, broke into enthusiastic applause. They liked Bjorn's impromptu wave. They were being entertained.

Zor smiled and nodded for Bjorn to continue.

Bjorn cleared his throat and announced, "When I arrived in Brio, I was unconscious, so I could not have killed Charlie Horse. The guard appointed to keep me in my quarters was the same one who guarded Charlie Horse next door. He could attest to the fact that I am innocent, but I now understand that he has been dismissed by Zor and can no longer be called and questioned, or even confirm my unconscious state. Nor can he confirm that I never left my room. I do realize, however, that what the people of Brio want to know is who, in fact, did kill Charlie Horse."

He took several steps toward the transparent wall, which blocked the gathering crowds from pouring into the courtroom.

As he approached, the crowds backed away, shrieking delightedly.

The jury started to talk amongst themselves.

One jury member stood up and announced, "Prisoner, if you were in your room, you have no way to point an accusing finger at another resident of Brio. You are the outsider."

Bjorn pointed back at the accusing juror and said, "The key is in the angle of the Brio cameras."

Zor blurted out, "And what possible significance could the position of the cameras have?"

Bjorn replied to Zor, "If I may call upon my guardian, Pat Seeds, who has brought in the footage, I can demonstrate…"

Zor nodded and beckoned for Pat Seeds, who hesitantly entered the courtroom, then displayed visual footage on the transparent wall.

The crowds outside clapped, pleased, as they stepped forward to see the replayed series of moving images taken from the visual recall devices inside Charlie's room.

Bjorn continued, "Oh, mighty Zor, is it not immediately obvious who killed Charlie Horse?"

Zor frowned and snorted, "This is boring. We have already seen this image. Projecting it onto the public observation wall is not entertaining." Zor crossed his arms and pursed his lips.

The jury, now seeing Zor's reaction, started to boo. Watson's balloon image looked as if his eyes were closing, weighed down by the tedium of the proceedings.

Watson's balloon head bounced a couple of times as it floated to Zor and sighed, "It exhausts me to make each city feel as if they are my one and only stop. Wrap this up. I must nap before I perform tonight."

Bjorn interrupted and spoke to the balloon judge directly, "Your lofty Watson-ness, may I beseech you to indulge me only a moment longer before we wrap up this trial for today. I wish to entertain your residents."

The crowds recoiled as if Bjorn had offended some law of decorum by speaking to Watson without first being addressed.

The Watson balloon looked up, then floated to Bjorn and said, "Perhaps it is best if you resume at a later date. This is a good cliffhanger."

Bjorn, ignoring Watson, addressed the

Jury of the Glass Courtroom without getting the official swish of approval from Zor. The crowd outside the transparent wall giggled with nervous delight over the upset.

Bjorn announced to the jury, "We have convened in this Glass Courtroom of Brio to uncover who killed Charlie Horse. Am I right?"

The crowds cheered.

Bjorn, realizing his bonds had been released, abruptly stood up and began to walk about as he testified, adding theatrically, "And if you convict the wrong man, that means you leave a murderer free to walk amongst you. Will you feel safe and entertained then? Or will you feel in danger and unable to trust your neighbor?"

The tone of the crowd now changed. They had not thought of that before.

Another jury member spoke up, "It is not possible that a local would destroy one of our own. The guilty one must be an outsider."

"Why?" Bjorn shot back.

The juror could not answer Bjorn.

The crowds outside the transparent wall now started to furtively glance around amongst themselves. They appeared confused, even a bit frightened. Bjorn wanted a reaction and he was getting it.

Bjorn continued boldly, "The guard discovered Charlie Horse's body that morning."

All eyes refocused on the transparent wall projection.

It showed the interior of Charlie's room as the guard opened the door and then raced to Charlie's limp body.

The image froze to indicate a time lapse.

A moment passed and then the image resumed moving to show the guard entering with Zor and pointing to Charlie's corpse.

The replayed footage showed Zor shaking his head with sympathy.

Bjorn spoke as the visual recall image jumped back in time to replay the actual act of murder.

Bjorn continued to present his observations. "It appears as if Charlie Horse was killed by an invisible intruder who held an invisible knife." He pointed to the large image, "but here, you can see a shadow." He gestured to another frozen image of Charlie Horse and said, "while here you see Charlie's own blood reveals the outline of the knife, and who..."

Instantly, Zor, waving his arms wildly, confronted the jury. "This has been done! We do not need to see it again! Shut down the visual recording playback!" Zor spun about to face Bjorn, and commanded, "Court is dismissed. We will resume at my next visit."

Bjorn took this chance to race straight to the Watson balloon and,

hesitating only a moment, punched it.

The entire jury, astonished, could only gape at this sudden outburst, and at the now bobbing Watson Bonitor balloon, a mix of a monitor to project Watson's image, but with the loft of a balloon.

Watson's image flickered off and his voice cried out, "I can't see. I can't hear. Zor! Fix the feed. What is going on. Can you hear me? Am I still visible?"

Zor, aghast turned to Bjorn, "What are you doing? This wasn't part of the contract!"

Bjorn raced to the transparent wall and addressed the crowds loudly so they could hear him.

"The killer wore a covering which the visual recordings could not detect. Charlie Horse didn't go mad. Charlie was murdered by a three dimensional being."

Zor worked furiously to retrieve Watson's feed back into the balloon so his boss, Watson, could see what was transpiring in the courtroom.

Zor tried to shout over Bjorn's voice. "Amusing theory, but not very sportsmanlike. You are using the defense of," and Zor changed his voice, "It was all a dream and then we all woke up."

The Jury followed suit and broke from their stony faces into laughter. Then, as if on cue, they stopped and then returned their unsmiling gaze to Bjorn Esterday.

Pat Seeds timidly asked, "Prisoner, who or what wore the covering which shielded their image from being recorded on the Visual Recall devices?"

Bjorn reversed the VR and replayed the portion of the footage where Charlie Horse got out of bed. He explained to the crowds, "The knife which was used to kill Mr. Horse is covered in the same cloaking material as the killer himself."

Zor interjected, "Or herself!"

"We know," Bjorn reiterated, "that the blood from Charlie's wounds is what coated and then revealed the shape of the knife." Then he walked to the other side of the image and added, "All this time we have been focused on the figure of Charlie Horse. Over here, on the seemingly vacant blank wall, you can barely see it, but it is there..."

Zor leaned in and squinted at where Bjorn was pointing, asking, "Are you pointing to a...a..." The Watson head was now re-engaged, and the image of Watson blinked back onto the balloon surface.

Bjorn finished Zor's sentence, "to a reflection in Charlie's mirror."

A juror stood up, "Why would a mirror pick up a reflection which the Visual Recall could not?"

Bjorn smiled, "The mirror was tinted. Although the camera cannot pick up on the fabric, the reflected image of the cloaked figure degraded the properties of the cloaking fabric so that the reflected and tinted image could be captured on the Visual Recall or VR. The tint altered the properties of the fabric allowing it to be recorded."

The floating head of Watson looked perplexed as the head floated closer to the murder scene. The jury and the crowds became very quiet.

Bjorn continued, "The reflection shows flowing robes such as yours, Zor," Bjorn stated.

Suddenly all eyes locked onto Zor.

Bjorn, now breaking his oath to not touch, yanked on Zor's sleeve revealing the lining which was of an oddly different pattern.

The Jury, and all those outside the glass wall, looked onto the monitors and noticed that the portion which revealed Zor's fabric lining was not transmitting to the monitors, as if that portion of his arm was invisible. Was Zor's fabric detected by the visual recorders or not?

Bjorn asked, "How many times have you been in Brio, invisible to everyone including your boss, Watson-head, over there?"

The crowds now started to applaud, well entertained by this new twist.

But then, they slowly realized who was being accused. It was their protector. The one who upheld the laws of Brio.

Zor!

Zor snapped back at Bjorn, "You lie! This courtroom is about justice!" He addressed the jury, "The prisoner lies!"

Bjorn continued, "I am quite a bit taller than you, Zor, and the height of the man in that room, which you can see over there..." Bjorn pointed to the murder scene, again. "The top of his head is also covered by a splatter of blood, establishing the murderer's height. The man's size is ... your height, Zor! Not mine! So even if I were conscious that night, which I was not, only you could have killed Charlie Horse! You! The keeper of peace and justice in this biosphere of Brio."

Bjorn turned to Pat, "The tinted mirror. Go! Stand next to Zor." Pat, holding the tinted mirror, scurried to hover at Zor's side.

Bjorn announced to the jury, "You remember that mirror had been in Charlie's room..."

Then Bjorn grabbed a Visual Recall device, which was being used to monitor the happenings of the court, and pointed it at the Jury.

The Jury's image now appeared on the transparent wall. Then, Bjorn pointed the Visual Recall at Zor, who still had the lining of his robe exposed.

Zor was visible, but the lining of his robe seemed to make his arm disappear in the projected image on the wall. Bjorn zoomed in on a portion Hof his arm which was also reflected in the tinted mirror.

The crowds could see an outline in the mirror, but the portion of Zor's arm, covered by the lining of his upturned sleeve, looked invisible.

Bjorn announced to the jury, "Did you sign up to live in this underwater paradise knowing your Zor, the protector of Brio, can turn invisible at any time and kill one of you?"

Bjorn pressed a button and the image of Zor was outlined up on the wall. Then that outline was super-imposed onto the moment when Charlie Horse was killed. The images were a match for Zor's height and face profile.

Yet another juror stood, but now addressed Zor.

"You promised me I'd find love, lose weight, get rich, and never be lonely again. Instead, you are using us for sport? To kill when you wish?"

The crowds started to bubble with the vehemence of molten lava slowly oozing, but ready to erupt.

Another yelled, "You said my life would be sweet as candy, but your caramel apple has a rotten core of manipulation!"

The Visual Recall screens chugged away until a fully digitized image of Zor was presented on the VR. Zor stood in front of the deceased Charlie Horse, in the spot where the invisible intruder had stood.

Another shouted, "I want a refund!"

The jury abruptly started to move toward Zor as a single unit.

The crowd outside the transparent wall began to push their way into the courtroom.

The Watson balloon shouted, "Order, order, order!" but the noisy crowds would not listen, would not be stopped.

In the confusion, Pat Seeds grabbed Bjorn's wrist and pulled Bjorn toward one of the side-exits leading out of the courtroom.

The crowds, transfixed, stared up at the ongoing wall re-enactment, this time to watch a new portion of the footage where one sees Bjorn Esterday, unconscious, being pulled in from the portal chute when he first arrived.

They watched as Bjorn's limp unconscious form was dragged past Charlie's room, placed in the room next door, well after the murder of Charlie Horse had occurred.

As Pat and Bjorn raced away down the now empty hallways, they heard the crowds behind them chanting, "games, games, games."

Pat Seeds pulled Bjorn into an alcove and said, "You have proven your innocence to me. You punched judge Watson. You accused Zor of murder. I've never seen the residents react with such violence. You have upset the balance! Are you sure you want to risk a trip to the surface? Would you rather humble yourself and apologize to Zor, in hopes he will show you leniency?"

"Uh. Not apologizing to anybody," Bjorn replied. "I need to surface. Get me to the portal chute."

5 CHAPTER 18: (2030) BRIO: ESCAPE POD: PAT AND BJORN TRY TO ESCAPE FROM BRIO

Pat Seeds zipped into a small rarely used corridor, closely followed by Bjorn, as they both ran through the labyrinth of Brio's winding hallways.

Bjorn was finding it difficult to catch his breath as he tried to keep up. "Don't you ever get tired, Pat?" he wheezed.

"I am sorry I never had time to show you my secret room," Pat explained while slipping through another narrow passage.

"Secret room?" Bjorn asked while trying to avoid bumping his head along internal ceiling pipes and wires.

"Yes. I've mentioned it before, but you were in too much of a rush to listen to me. The main entrance has been blocked off with odds and ends. Storage..." Pat explained, "Bit by bit, I've cleaned up one room to reveal a lovely view of the water. When I discharge food, I can see the sea life feasting. It is very satisfying."

"Why was it blocked off in the first place?" Bjorn asked.

Pat glanced back quickly as they hurried, not daring to pause. "It used to be a docking station for two pods. One was lost some time ago and the other hasn't been used in ages. I used the empty dock to discharge food bits for the water creatures. Dolphins. Sometimes whales. Fish. So much magic here... "

Bjorn panted as he trailed behind, "I just care about getting out of this bubble."

Pat raced to the portal chute door by slipping through the next narrow corridor, dashed across a wide hallway to the portal chute room, tugged at the handle and pressed a button near the door.

The door did not move.

Pat quickly stepped to what appeared to be a manual override lever and tugged at that.

Nothing.

"It seems quite peaceful in this area..." Pat whispered hopefully. "Maybe this is a sign that you should stay, Bjorn Esterday."

Bjorn stared at her, speechless.

"All right, then..." Pat took a deep breath and continued, "...here is the portal chute. But, there is a series of steps to open it. First I must..."

Bjorn ignored Pat as soon as he recognized the indicator for an override lever. He reached past Pat and grabbed at the lever with his powerful hands, yanking hard.

Pat cried, "No! Stop! Stop!"

Bjorn released the lever, now slightly bent, and in frustration rammed his large frame against the side of the portal door while chanting to himself, "Open, open, open you blasted door!"

But it did not respond to Bjorn's brute force.

"Bjorn Esterday Otto Mattick!" Pat cried, "You must cease immediately!"

Bjorn replied, "I didn't get this close to escaping to let some stuck door keep me trapped here."

Agitated, Pat exclaimed, "Be patient! Your frustration is preventing you from...."

"What?"

Pat Seeds admonished, "That door only opens when you follow specific procedures. No shortcuts. Rushing the process will cause harm to others. You must not force destiny. But, I understand. One bad choice can change your destiny. I made a bad choice once...you think it will be for a little while, then the consequences become...forever." Pat sighed as if in a dreamy state of recollection.

"Then what is this process?" Bjorn demanded desperately, trying to snap Pat back to the present.

Pat, staring at him wide-eyed, replied, "I forgot. I know it's around here somewhere."

Frustration flashed in Bjorn's eyes as he yanked on the door, "I was kidnapped...Don't I have a right to get out of here? Don't you?"

Bjorn continued to force the door.

Unexpectedly, the door contacts sparked and eased open about three inches, then stopped. Just enough to get a hand through, but not much else.

Pat gaped at Bjorn and then at the partially open door and replied softly, "No. I don't have a right to get out. I chose to hide in Brio."

Bjorn started to tug at the opening to make it wider, "Hide? What could you have possibly done on the surface, Pat Seeds, which would warrant cutting yourself off and hiding in an underwater garden?"

Pat explained without emotion, "With a dented inner door, the seal won't be air tight. You know Watson has cut back on maintenance repairs. That door could leak, now. I'll have to create a sign to warn the others."

"We don't have time to write signs, Pat," Bjorn protested as Pat found a pen and scribbled "Do Not Use" on the door itself.

Pat firmly replied, "I also have a sense of justice, Bjorn Esterday, and I am obligated to warn others to not open this portal until it can be repaired... Zor usually remains in Brio for several days, so it will be fixed before he needs to leave."

Hearing the approaching crowds, Bjorn snapped, "Hey, I'm sorry I broke that portal door seal. I was thinking of me. You thought of others. But, Pat, the Brio-crats are going to want to silence me after that trial. Maybe you for helping me....is there another way out? Your secret room? You said there was a pod there, right?"

Pat did not respond but strode to the blank wall, smacked it, and the panel fell open, revealing another corridor inside the walls.

Turning away from the portal chute, Pat evaluated Bjorn's large frame and then the size of the panel. Pat stepped in, beckoning Bjorn to follow.

Bjorn picked up the loose panel and replaced it to cover the opening behind him, then he and Pat entered these new passages behind the bank of walls.

Pat explained as they wended their way through the narrow corridor inside the walls, "I overheard once that there is a different ruling power. On the surface. Called the Twins."

Focusing on his goal, Bjorn agreed, "Twins. Yeah. The epitome of power by force."

Pat continued calmly, "The Twins had invested in this place assuming it would be a station used for military exercises...but with the glass walls, it was not exactly a fortress impervious to attacks... It was originally built to simulate living in outer space..."

"Outer space. As in stars and planets?" Bjorn's brow furrowed.

Pat explained, "For astronauts. To train them. But, when the military option wasn't viable, they gave it to Watson to create the Brio....as you call it....a time share."

Bjorn, impatiently asked, "Is this information going to help me get out of here?"

Pat replied while increasing their pace, "My secret room used to deploy water pods, so Watson had Zor block it off since there was no need for any resident to ever leave. Only the portal chute would be used to transport Zor and new residents from the surface. I was one of the first residents of Brio."

Impatiently, Bjorn asked, "Great. Are we getting close to the escape pods?"

Pat turned back saying, "I don't even know if the remaining pod works or not."

Hearing the crowds echoing against the inner walls, Bjorn could detect they were shouting something else, now "Mattick, Mattick..."

Pat paused to listen before turning a corner into what looked like a huge pipe and said blandly, "Resident programming. They are no longer angry at Zor. They are now angry at you."

Bjorn followed Pat, who stepped into a larger room with two heavy doors each equipped with a thick underwater glass window. One exit had a pod attached. The other did not.

Pat explained, "The empty dock is the one I use to feed the fishies." Then Pat pointed to the main door, which had a small window in it.

Bjorn peered out and saw various odds and ends piled up against the door.

"Some storage items still block the entrance from the hallway, so I think you will have time," Pat explained.

Pat approached the window.

Sea creatures, large and small, clustered around, obviously associating the sight of Pat with food soon to be expelled to them.

"I'm ready to leave timeshare Atlantis nightmare," Bjorn muttered under his breath, "How do we activate the pod?"

Pat continued with placid patience, "It's not a portal chute, which is pre-programmed to push you to the surface via a tube. If you use the pod, you will have to navigate it yourself."

"Fine. Navigate. How hard can that be?" Bjorn jeered.

Pat opened the inner door to reveal the entrance to the pod. Out the window of the pod, Bjorn could see the sea life had started to obscure the pod window exposed to the water due to it's lack of use.

Pat pointed to the pod interior. "That is the seat. I think this button opens and closes this door hatch to keep the water out. That, over there, steers the pod...I think....and that dial...maybe.... I think tells you how far below sea level you are. I am not an expert. You will figure it out. I would advise that you ascend slowly so you avoid decompression problems."

Bjorn added, "Yeah. Would be a shame to escape a Brio execution only to die from ascending to the surface too fast. Ok, Pat. If you steer, I'll monitor the controls. Good thing there are two chairs."

Pat stepped into the pod, looked out one of the portal windows, and pointed off into the sea at a large box=shaped structure anchored in the sea bed some distance outside.

Pat said, "I think that building over there monitors the pumps and irrigation distribution system which splits out the oxygen molecules and pumps them inside Brio. It also houses the saline converter, which generates fresh water for the gardens and the visitors." Pat sighed, "Oh, look, the dolphins are coming. They expect a feeding, I'm sure."

Bjorn leaned in, quickly peering at the instruments inside the pod, then pulled back.

He looked around as he heard the distant echoes of an angry crowd, some chanting "Zor, Zor..." and others chanting "Mattick, Mattick..."

Bjorn nervously glanced at Pat and said, "I don't think we will have time for a feeding today, Pat."

Pat patiently nodded and understood.

"Get in," Pat offered to Bjorn as Pat stepped out of the pod to allow Bjorn to slip by. "See if the Pod fits."

Pat pointed to the small chairs inside the pod.

Bjorn gingerly stepped inside and was barely able to fit in the seats, as they were built for much smaller people.

Pat stepped away and pushed a button on the wall, which activated an old fashioned microphone. Pat said, "Oh, I think this is a voice transfer. Can you hear me inside the pod?"

Bjorn replied, "If you come into the pod and sit next to me, we won't need mics. Just get in the pod."

Pat returned to the pod door, but did not get in as Bjorn beckoned. After a brief hesitation, Pat tossed in an old model HIB, which landed in Bjorn's lap.

As Bjorn picked up the HIB asking, "What is this?" Pat slammed a button inside the Pod door and pulled away as the Pod door rapidly sealed Bjorn insiPat smiled at Bjorn from outside the pod.

Then, Pat raced to the microphone on the wall.

Alarmed, Bjorn grabbed the HIB with one hand and tried to figure out how to open the door with the other.

Pat depressed the button on the mic's control panel so Bjorn could hear Pat from within the pod.

"My HIB is waterproof," Pat called. "Please, before you go home, could you find where I am?"

"I know where you are," Bjorn yelled back, trying to locate the mic from inside the pod. Finding it, he shouted, "Pat, you are coming with me! Pat!" Bjorn shouted. "Open this pod door and get in. They'll kill you for helping me!"

Pat glanced around the room and saw air tanks and diving suits over to the side of the control room in which Pat now stood. "I hope you have enough air to get to the surface. I'm sorry you didn't have time to get supplies."

Pat searched the corner of the room, which had air tanks and wet suits. None of which were inside Bjorn's pod.

Suddenly there was a loud metallic groaning. Both Pat and Bjorn felt a jolt, which unsteadied them.

"Pat. Get in!" Bjorn shouted from inside the pod pounding on the door, uncertain how to open it, "Get in!"

Pat scrambled for the mic, which fell off the wall as the Brio structure jolted again. Pat announced to Bjorn, "I think Zor must have left through that portal chute. I think that is why the structure is..."

Bjorn replied, "Why would Zor endanger all of Brio when you had the sign not to use it?"

Pat replied, "To save himself... Maybe because he was surprised that you changed the rules of the game, Bjorn Esterday. I don't think either Watson or Zor thought you could figure out how Charlie Horse really died. But you took the time to prove to me you were innocent. I appreciate that, but now if..."Zor left through the portal chute you damaged, then, Brio might flood. "

Bjorn cried, "Pat. Open the pod door and get in."

Pat mused, "How can I think of saving myself when all the residents are in as much jeopardy as I am should Zor's departure cause a flood?"

Bjorn snapped in a panic, "I didn't mean to break the seal. You have to leave with me. I didn't mean to endanger all of Brio. This pod is our only chance! We can get to the surface and summon help to rescue the others. Get in!"

Pat replied calmly, "I think Longfellow is close by because he is hoping she will return, but she was never here. It was me, not her." Pat seemed to relish a memory and said, "I had my birthday in Rough-N-Ready, before I met Longfellow. Find Longfellow, then find me. I think Brio may flood, now."

Frantically, Bjorn searched for a way to open the pod door, but Pat was controlling operations from the outside, overriding any button Bjorn was frantically pressing.

"Pat Seeds!" Bjorn yelled, but his voice

was muffled from inside the pod.

One button Bjorn pressed allowed him to hear what was happening inside the glass courtroom. The angry chants were now replaced by a cacophony of confused panicky cries. Bjorn's heart raced with frantic frustration.

Pat Seeds calmly activated buttons from inside the secret room, swaying like a practiced sailor on stormy seas as the groaning structure of Brio started to move.

Bjorn heard alarms going off.

The pod screen now leapt to life and flashed warnings.

Bjorn looked out into the murky depths through one of the water-side pod portholes. His heart began to race. His mouth went dry. He forced himself to breath steadily as he tried to figure out how to respond.

He could see in the distance that

square structure which Pat said was the underwater saline converter building. It started to bubble.

Pat, now satisfied that the pre-launch checks had been sequentially observed, replied through the mic, "You were impatient, but you are forgiven, my innocent friend."

Then, Pat pressed the launch button, jarring Bjorn back into one of the seats. The pod shot out with a whoosh into the quiet waters surrounding Brio.

8 What Just Happened?

Bjorn surprised the stale Glass Courtroom of Brio by using his honed investigative reporting skills to piece together a puzzle the perpetrators thought nobody could figure out.

Bjorn was surprised that he got Pat Seed's trust, and then Pat's help.

Bjorn realized the Brio courtroom was much more about drawing in viewers than about true justice. When he could not use logic or truth to set himself free, he tried something else.

However, Bjorn's escape plans did not go as expected. What will happen to Bjorn, and where is the real 'Otto Mattick'?

9 Did You Know...

In this story, Bjorn Esterday, known as Otto Mattick in Brio, refers to Brio as "Atlantis" and in particular the "Atlantis nightmare".

Did you know Atlantis means "daughter of Atlas". In Greek mythology, Maia (sometimes Maias) was a daughter of Atlas and Pleione. In a grotto of Mt. Cyllene in Arcadia, she and Zeus produced Hermes. She also adopted a son, Arcas, whose father was Zeus and mother Callisto.

Atlantis has been used in our language since the 1730s to refer to a fictional island-nation which, in myth, was submerged under water.

Some say the original story of Atlantis

was referenced in Plato's writings around the year 360 B C, in particular "Timaeus" and "Critias".

Critias appears to be a work which was never quite finished. Some say Critias and Charmides and even Plato's relatives comprised the "Thirty Tyrants"(οἱ τριάκοντα τύραννοι).

The Thirty Tyrants was a group of possibly Spartan oligarchs which sponsored a coup around the Peloponnesian War (404 to 403 BC), which wreaked havoc all over Greece, costing countless lives and destroying civic life and contstructs.

Many wanted to destroy and eradicate those who lived in Athens.

Spartans (sometimes called the Lacedaemonians from around the 5th century) were from Lacedaemon (now Laconia). This location was on the banks of the Eurotas River in Laconia, in south-eastern Peloponnese.

The Thirty Tyrants were rulers who governed Athens for about 8 months. They ruled by brute force and fear. Later, this style of rule by intimidation was looked down upon by residents of Athens. The Spartan "rule by the few" was no longer considered an acceptable governance style.

For three generations thereafter, "rule by the people" was considered the wiser and more productive alternative.

The Spartans instead struck a bargain that required the residents of Athens to remove walls and fortresses from around Piraeus, withdraw magistrates from Poleis territories, recall all exiles, and remove any settlements from the Poleis regions.

They were to also declare all loyalty to have the same "friends and enemies" as the ruling Spartans (Lacedaemonians), as well as restructure their laws to favor an oligarchy or "rule by the few".

The Thirty delayed crafting a constitution and instead wanted an interim government, which would provide them the freedom to get rid of opponents and get rid of laws with which they disagreed.

The writings of Timaeus were intended to demonstrate a morality play to show ethical choices. In the writings of Timaeus, the Republic values virtuous choices made in an individual's life despite difficult and tempting worldly influences to behave non-virtuously.

In Plato's writings, those who behave with "good" actions, eventually have a "good" reward. Likewise, those who behave with "bad" intentions or indulge in vices, will reap the negative consequence of those choices.

In Plato's stories of virtue versus vice, or good versus evil takes place with the backdrop of an exotic Atlantis.

Some say the people of Atlantis evidenced selfish, venal, deviant, greedy, self-centered, bullying, petty, and morally bankrupt behavior which was so distasteful that the Greek gods sent "one terrible night of fire and earthquakes" which caused Atlantis to sink forever into the sea to silence the evil and allow good to grow once more.

10 Vocabulary

This fictional series introduces some words unique to this world. Also used are standard terms which we encourage you to investigate in a dictionary for your own edification. Consolidated full list of vocabulary for all GONE books is located in the Conversation Station supplemental book.

Bonitor: This is a balloon monitoring system whereby the supervisors project their own two-dimensional faces onto the three-dimensional inflated floating balloon, which is able to move around with remote controls. The Bonitor floats along to monitor staff while projecting their images onto the balloon so the boss does not have to physically be in the room, but checks in on staff remotely.

Watsonness This is a term used in Brio. It is used as in "Your lofty Watsonness". This term is created to stroke the ego of the man who holds power by instilling authoritarian fear in his subject Watson. By addressing him in this manner, a submissive and fearful subjects, who know they are disposable, and also acknowledge there is no word which can describe how great this leader is, so they create a word or title out of his own name.

It is generally done with such exaggerated pomp and circumstance that to an outsider it may seem sarcastic, overly dramatic, or over-done, yet the recipient, Watson, for example, demands such adoration and does not care if it is sincere or not.

Glass Courtroom or **"Glass Court"** This is a term used in Brio to note that the court-case is intended to be as dramatic as possible to provide entertainment to the jury and all those outside the glass wall looking in.

The term indicates that the lives of the residents of Brio are so devoid of mental stimulation that they derive entertainment and experiences which are so extreme it would awaken their senses and make them "feel alive".

In this story, the example is the trial of Bjorn Esterday, who has been burdened by being forced to assume the identity of Otto Mattick.

The jury and onlookers do not know if Otto Mattick is guilty or innocent of the murder of Charlie Horse, but the trial is absurd and not intended to discover the truth.

This is not a genuine court-trial. It is a mere imitation or a glass obscured version of a real trial.

In this story we do not know if Charlie Horse was killed to provide entertainment to the people or not. It is possible Charlie Horse was eliminated because Charlie was a threat to Watson. Did Charlie Horse unearth information which would jeopardize Watson's status and position? Did Charlie Horse seek vengeance because a loved one was conned by Watson?

The whole purpose of the trial is to provide entertainments to the onlookers and possibly be an excuse for Zor, Watson, or any other person in power to quietly get rid of the people they do not like.

This is not a trial of justice. This is not an exercise to find out who is guilty or innocent. Watson's goal is to make this dramatized "trial" as engaging as possible so that many people will watch it from outside the glass wall.

What matters is the show and number of interested viewers. Not the truth. Not justice. Not if anybody innocent gets hurt. Not even if the wrong man gets convicted.

The assumption is anybody outside

Brio is fair game and can be slaughtered as nobody inside the group could ever be blamed for wrongdoing....even if they actually were guilty.   In Brio,   the collective group would deny it to others and even to themselves.

Visual Recall devices (VR)- These devices replay back supposedly recorded footage, but it is difficult to tell if these images are genuine and are essentially used as a prop to create a story to be played out in a Glass Courtroom.

In this story, Bjorn proves how a false image was generated to cast doubt into the "evidence" presented via the VR. This is not virtual reality.

Portal chute This is the door way which connects an underwater submersible vehicle or other connecting bridge-like contrivances to the main door of Brio.

Brio-crats: This is a term used for the bureaucrats who are in Brio, thinking they are persecuted, whining and bemoaning their plight, when in fact, they are the bullies, whose actions cause confusion and delays to ferreting out the truth.

Atlantis nightmare: This is a term Bjorn used on Brio to reference they mythological city of fictional underwater city of Atlantis, which was supposed to have been a paradise. Yet, because of Bjorn's negative experiences, he calls Brio the Atlantis Nightmare.

ABOUT Wynter Sommers

Wynter Sommers is the pseudonym for an American writing team, which harnesses multiple skills in technology, research, history and education. Formally trained with a PhD in Education, Wynter Sommers blends academic classroom experience, with corporate sophistication, and a passion for developing more effective student insights through engaging storytelling.

Wynter Sommers has a heart to inspire creativity and develop critical thinking skills, all to encourage readers to make wise choices in life.

Wynter Sommers takes each story and weaves the plot with classic gripping elements, which endure throughout repeated readings, revealing new meanings each time the story is explored. The small choices a reader makes in real life could have a lasting effect in future generations. This set of stories shows the origin of not just Bjorn Esterday and Sarah Paradise, but of their ancestors and the sort of world which was established, which unfolded in each generation until Bjorn and Sarah met.

It is rewarding to learn of heartfelt, thought provoking conversations taking place globally about the characters of these books. Should the reader be presented with extraordinary circumstances, it is the sincerest wish that they act with honor, truth and integrity to overcome obstacles in real life whilst the reader hones skills of self-reliance and collaborative teamwork despite barriers outside of the reader's control. Wynter Sommers hopes you enjoy the other ***Bjorn Esterday Was not Born Yesterday*** stories in this series.